# PIXIE TRICKS

## The Angry Elf

# Catch all of the Pixie Tricks adventures!

# PIXIE TRICKS

## The Angry Elf

· by ·
**TRACEY
WEST**

A
**LITTLE APPLE**
PAPERBACK

SCHOLASTIC INC.
New York  Toronto  London  Auckland  Sydney
Mexico City  New Delhi  Hong Kong

*Book design by Dawn Adelman*

ISBN 0-439-17981-5

Cover illustration by James Bernardin
Interior and sticker illustrations by Thea Kliros

12 11 10 9 8 7 6 5 4 3 2 1                    0 1 2 3 4 5/0

Printed in the U.S.A.                          40
First Scholastic printing, November 2000

For my wonderful family.
Thanks for putting up with
this angry elf for so
many years.
— T.W.

# ·:· Contents ·:·

Sprite is a Pixie Tricker,

Who was sent by the fairy queen.

He's after fourteen pixies.

They're troublesome and mean!

Sprite asked for help from Violet,

A clever little girl.

She'll help him trick the pixies,

And send them to their world.

So far they have tricked five pixies,

With nine more left to go.

Will Sprite and Violet trick them?

Keep reading and you'll know!

# Chapter One
# A Day Off?

"I can't find it anywhere!"

Violet Briggs looked on her bed. She flipped over pillows.

Violet opened a dresser drawer. Inside, a tiny fairy was curled up in a soft pair of socks. The fairy opened his eyes and yawned.

"Is it time to wake up?" asked Sprite, the fairy. "I'm so sleepy!"

"You have been sleeping all morning!"
Violet said a little crossly.

Sprite stretched his rainbow-colored wings.
He flew out of the drawer and sat on the
dresser. His green legs dangled over the side.

"Sorry!" Sprite said. "I'm worn out from
looking for escaped pixies yesterday. I
wanted to get some rest before we started
today."

Violet sighed. Her life had changed so much since the day she met Sprite. He had come through a magical door in the oak tree in her backyard.

Sprite had explained that fourteen pixies had escaped from his world. It was Sprite's job to trick them and send them back. He had asked Violet to help him.

Violet had agreed. Since then, they had tricked five pixies together.

But today Violet needed a break.

"I'm not looking for pixies today," she told Sprite. "I'm going to Brittany's birthday party."

"That's right!" Sprite said. "I forgot. When are you going?"

"I'm not sure," Violet said. "I can't find the invitation. I've been looking for it every-where."

Just then, someone knocked on Violet's door.

"It's Dad," said Violet's father.

Quickly, Sprite hid behind a teddy bear. Violet opened the door.

Violet's dad had a mop of blond hair and green eyes. He was carrying a wrapped-up present.

"Brittany's mom left a message," explained Mr. Briggs. "She said the party starts at one."

"Great!" Violet said.

Mr. Briggs shook the present. "Your mom wrapped this before she went to work," he said. "What did you get Brittany?"

"It's really cool!" Violet said, excited. "It's a Dancing Dolphin Waterfall. When you turn the key, it lights up and the waterfall turns on. Then dolphins dance up and down."

Mr. Briggs handed Violet the box. Then he ruffled her brown hair.

"Let me know when you're ready to go to the party. I'll give you a ride," he said.

Violet kissed his cheek. "Thanks, Dad."

Mr. Briggs closed the door. Sprite flew out from behind the teddy bear.

"Birthdays are fun!" he said. "Can I come?"

Violet sat down on her bed. "I wish you could," she said. "But somebody might see you. You know I have to keep you a secret."

"I know," Sprite said with a sigh. He sounded disappointed.

Suddenly, a boy burst into the room. He had sandy-blond hair and wore jeans and a sweatshirt.

"Are we tricking any pixies today?" he asked.

"Leon, can't you knock?" Violet asked her cousin. Leon and his mom lived downstairs from Violet. He was always hanging around. He even knew about Sprite.

Leon had helped them trick some pixies. Of course, Leon thought he was the best Pixie Tricker ever.

Sprite flew up to Leon. "Violet is going to Brittany's birthday party. I have to stay here."

Leon flopped down on the floor. "I'm bored," he complained.

Sprite fluttered his wings, excited. "Maybe you and I could look for pixies," he said.

"Yeah," Leon said. "Why not?"

The idea of Leon and Sprite out on their own made Violet nervous. Even though

Sprite was a Royal Pixie Tricker, he was new at his job. He made a lot of mistakes.

And Leon — well, Leon was just Leon.

"Why don't you wait until I get back from the party?" Violet asked. "I won't be long. Then we can look for Hinky Pink."

Hinky Pink was a fairy who could change the weather. Sprite and Violet had been trying to trick him from the start. So far, they'd had no luck.

Sprite and Leon looked at each other.

"I guess we can wait for you," Sprite said finally. "Don't be long!"

"I'll be back as soon as the party's over!" Violet said. "I'm going to have a good time at this party. And no fairy is going to spoil it!"

## Chapter Two
# Toy Trouble

"Violet, you're late!" Brittany said.

Violet looked at the clock on the wall. It wasn't even one o'clock yet.

"But I thought the party started at one," she said.

"It started at twelve," Brittany told her. "We already had food and cake. Now I'm going to open presents. Come on!"

Brittany led Violet to the living room. Balloons and streamers hung everywhere. They were Brittany's favorite color, orange.

Violet's other good friend, Tina, called her over.

"Sit next to me, Violet!" Tina said, pointing to a spot on the floor.

Violet put her gift on a pile of presents. She sat down and looked around.

Sitting on the couch were Maria and April, two girls from Brittany's ballet class. Next to them sat Jen and Kayla, two girls from school.

Brittany sat in a chair next to the presents. She picked up a box wrapped in pink.

"That's from me," said April.

Brittany opened the present. She took out a white music box. On top stood a tiny ballerina.

"Oh, it's so pretty!" Brittany said. She

turned the gold key on the side of the box. The girls waited to hear what tune it would play.

"*Mooooooo!*" was the noise that came out of the box. "*Moooooo!*"

April blushed. "It's supposed to play 'Beautiful Dreamer.'"

Brittany tried to smile. "That's okay. I, uh, I like cows."

"Open mine next," Tina said quickly. She handed Brittany a package wrapped in bright paper.

"I wonder what it is," Brittany said.

She tore off the paper. Underneath was a box with a round furry creature inside. The toy had big wiggly eyes.

"It's an electronic Fuzzy Pet," Tina explained.

"I know!" Brittany said, opening the box.

"Everyone is getting one. They're amazing. They talk to you and everything."

Brittany took out the Fuzzy Pet and pressed the button on its belly.

"Hi, I'm the Fuzzy Pet," said the toy.

Brittany smiled.

"Boy, your hair is a mess today!" the pet said.

The girls gasped.

"What did you say?" Brittany asked. She pressed the button again.

"You're so boring," said the Fuzzy Pet. "Nobody wants to play with you."

Brittany looked shocked. Tina's dark eyes filled with tears.

"Brittany, I'm so sorry!" she said. "There must be something wrong with it."

"It's all right," Brittany said. But she didn't sound like she meant it. "I bet my little brother will like it. He's always saying mean stuff like that."

Violet put her arm around Tina. "Don't feel bad. It wasn't your fault."

But Violet was worried. Something strange was going on. She could feel it.

Brittany opened the rest of her presents.

Maria gave her a sticker set. But none of the stickers were sticky!

Jen gave her a stuffed tiger. But it had a tiger's head and a duck's body!

Kayla gave her a Missy Model doll. But none of Missy's clothes fit!

Brittany tried to smile each time. But everyone knew she was disappointed.

Finally Brittany picked up Violet's gift.

Violet held her breath. The Dancing Dolphin Waterfall was the perfect gift for Brittany. There couldn't possibly be anything wrong with it.

Could there?

"Oh, Violet, this is just what I wanted!" Brittany said. "We have to try it out."

"Okay," Violet said nervously.

Brittany got a cup of water from the kitchen and poured it into the back of the waterfall.

The girls gathered around the toy. Brittany slowly turned the key.

*Splash!* Jets of cold water shot out of the toy. The water sprayed all over the room.

It soaked the furniture.

It soaked the decorations.

It soaked the party guests.

And of course, it soaked Brittany.

Brittany couldn't take it anymore.

"That's it!" she wailed. "This is the worst birthday party ever!"

# Chapter Three
## Fixit

When Violet got home, she heard noises in Leon's room.

"I'll come up later," she told her dad. "I need to talk to Leon."

Violet's wet shoes squished as she walked down the hall. She was in no mood to look for Hinky Pink today. Leon and Sprite would just have to wait.

Violet knocked on the door.

"Who is it?" Leon asked.

"It's Violet!" she said.

"Oh," said Leon. "Come in."

Violet opened the room. Then she gasped.

Leon and Sprite were a mess! They were covered with dirt, flour, and what looked like chocolate icing.

"What happened to you?" Violet asked.

Sprite tried to fly to Violet. But his wings were too sticky. He sank down on Leon's bed.

"Leon and I thought we might look for Hinky Pink without you," Sprite said weakly.

"Oh, no!" said Violet. "You didn't!"

Sprite nodded sheepishly. "We thought we'd go to the lake. We haven't tried there yet."

"But we didn't make it to the lake!" Leon

said. "Sprite threw his pixie dust and tried to get us there. And we landed in a cake in the bakery."

Sprite shrugged. "Cake. Lake. It's an honest mistake."

"Then we landed in the pet store. In a cage with a snake!" Leon said. "And next we landed right on top of a rake! And after that —"

"I get the picture," Violet said. "Are you okay?"

Violet wanted to be mad at them for going without her. But she couldn't. They looked so silly.

Sprite picked the last of the icing from his wings. He flew onto Violet's shoulder. "I know I'm not the best when it comes to pixie dust," he said. "But this was bad, even for me. I think something's wrong."

"Well, I *know* something's wrong!" Violet said. She told Sprite and Leon about Brittany's party. About the messed-up toys.

"That sounds like something Fixit would do!" Sprite cried. "I should have known that elf was in this world."

"An elf?" Violet asked. "Aren't elves supposed to be *good* at making toys?"

"They are," Sprite said. "But Fixit loves to fix it so that toys don't work the right way."

"Why does he do that?" Leon asked.

"Because kids don't care about all the hard work I do!"

Violet, Leon, and Sprite jumped at the sound of the strange voice. There was a puff of light, and a small pixie appeared in the room.

It was an elf. He was about half as tall as Violet. He had a white beard and a thin, pinched face. He wore a red cap on his head and buckled shoes on his feet. In his hand he carried a tiny hammer.

"Fixit!" Sprite cried. "What are you doing here?"

"I heard you talking about me," Fixit said. "It's time people know. I'm tired of working day and night to make toys. What happens?

You kids play with them once and throw them away. It's disgraceful."

"That's not true!" Violet said. "Not everyone treats their toys that way."

Fixit looked around Leon's room. His toys were all over the place.

"Look at this mess!" Fixit said. He glared at Leon. "You. Boy. Is this your room?"

Leon nodded, too afraid to speak.

"Is this the thanks I get for making toys?" Fixit asked. "You don't even care about them."

Fixit raised the hammer in front of him. He pointed it at a toy robot on the floor.

"Fixit Tixif!" Fixit yelled. A light like a lightning bolt flew out of the hammer. It hit the robot.

The robot sat on the floor. It stuck one thumb into its metal mouth.

"Waaah!" cried the robot. "I want my mommy!"

"That's much better!" Fixit said. "And now I've got to go. I've got more toys to fix!"

Before they could do anything to stop him, Fixit vanished.

Leon picked up the robot.

"Time to change my diaper," said the toy.

"Oh, brother," Leon said. "We've got to do something about that elf!"

# Chapter Four
## Applesauce Stew

That night, Violet and Sprite tried to find out more about Fixit. They looked in the *Book of Tricks.*

Queen Mab, the fairy queen, had given Sprite the book. It told how to trick all the escaped pixies.

Sprite turned the tiny pages. "Here it is," he said. "Fixit's pages."

On one page was a blank space where Fixit's picture should be. His picture would only appear once he was caught. On the other page was a rhyme.

Fixit is filled
with anger
and bile,
To trick this
elf, you must
make him smile.

Violet squinted to read it.

*"Fixit is filled with anger and bile,*
*To trick this elf,*
*you must make him smile.'"*

"Bile?" Sprite asked. "What's bile?"

"It must be something angry people have," Violet said. "But that's not the important part. What's important is that we have to make him smile."

Sprite fluttered around the room. "That can't be too hard!" he said, excited. "We could tell him a joke. Or tickle him. Or . . ."

Violet yawned.

"We can figure it out tomorrow," she said. "After school."

"All right," Sprite sighed. Violet watched him fly to her top dresser drawer. The little pixie curled up in a pair of socks and fell asleep.

The next day, Violet slipped Sprite into her desk just before class started.

Her teacher, Ms. Rose, faced the class.

"I'd like everyone to pass up their homework," she said. "I hope you all were able to answer the questions on page thirty of your science books."

Violet took the homework paper out of her backpack. Then she froze.

She had answered social studies questions, not science questions. She had done the wrong homework!

Other kids in the class looked worried, too. No one passed up their papers.

"What's the matter, class?" Ms. Rose asked.

Brittany raised her hand. "Ms. Rose, I did social studies homework, not science homework."

"Me, too!" other kids joined in.

Ms. Rose shook her head. "I'm not sure how this happened," she said. "Just pass up your papers. You can do the science home-work tonight."

Violet sighed, relieved. At least she wasn't the only one.

The rest of the morning went smoothly. When the lunch bell rang, Violet scooped up Sprite. She put him in her sweater pocket.

"Thank goodness," Sprite whispered to her. "I'm hungry."

But when they got to the lunchroom, something was wrong. Two of the lunch ladies were arguing.

"I said to put tomato sauce in that stew!" one woman said. "Not applesauce!"

"The message you left said applesauce!" said the other woman. "I'm sure!"

The lunch ladies stopped arguing when they noticed the students.

The first woman spoke. "You're in for a

special treat today, kids!" she said, trying to smile. "Applesauce stew!"

Violet looked at her friends Brittany and Tina. Applesauce stew?

Violet and her friends got their lunch and sat down. She picked at the mushy mess on her plate.

"I'm glad my mom packed me a banana," Brittany said.

Just then, the girls heard a laugh from the next table. Violet turned her head.

It was Evan Peters, a boy from her class. He was showing off his new yo-yo.

"Check it out," Evan said. "I can do all kinds of tricks with it."

Evan put the string around his finger. He threw the yo-yo.

The yo-yo rolled down to the floor.

Then the round part of the yo-yo flew off!

It bounced up. It knocked over Evan's milk and landed on his sandwich. The milk poured into Evan's lap.

His friends laughed.

But the yo-yo bounced again. It bounced into a bowl of applesauce stew. It bounced into every bowl of applesauce stew on the table!

"It's Fixit!" Violet said under her breath.

Violet saw her pocket wiggle. She knew Sprite wanted to know what was happening.

"Violet, look out!" Brittany cried.

Violet turned around again. The yo-yo was bouncing her way!

Violet reached for the yo-yo. She was too late. The yo-yo bounced into the stew in her bowl.

*Splash!* The soggy stew flew into Violet's face.

That didn't stop Violet. She reached out
and grabbed the yo-yo before it could
bounce again.

"Got it!" Violet yelled.

The kids in the lunchroom cheered.

Violet handed Evan the yo-yo.

"I guess it's broken," Evan said.

Violet didn't answer.

This was the second time she had been soaked in two days.

And it was all because of Fixit!

"Watch out, Fixit!" Violet muttered. "I'm going to trick you if it's the last thing I do!"

# Chapter Five
## The Fairy Lure

After school, Violet washed the last of the applesauce stew from her hair. Her mom helped her braid it into two neat braids. Then Violet went into her room and closed the door.

"Sprite, we need to do something about Fixit!" she cried.

Sprite flew up to her face. "You are as angry as that elf!" he said.

Violet tried to calm down. Being angry was no fun.

"To trick Fixit, we have to make him smile," she said. "I think we need to find out more about him."

"Good idea," Sprite said. "Uh, how do we do that?"

"I think we should find him and talk to him," Violet said. "He seemed to like talking to us."

"You mean complaining," Sprite said. "But you're right. We should find him."

Violet picked up a phone book she had gotten from her mom. "There are three toy stores in town. We can start there."

"Great!" Sprite said. He reached into his magic bag for some pixie dust. "We can go now!"

Violet looked at the clock. "It's almost

time for supper," she said. "We can't go running all over the place now."

Sprite landed on Violet's bed. The room was quiet for a little while.

Then Sprite sprang up. "I've got it!" he said. "We can bring Fixit to us!"

Sprite took out the *Book of Tricks*. He thumbed through the pages.

"Here it is!" Sprite said finally. "A fairy lure!"

Violet took the book from Sprite's hands. She looked at the page.

"These are just squiggles," Violet said.

"Look closer!" Sprite said impatiently.

Violet walked to her desk. She picked up a magnifying glass. Then she looked at the page again.

"They're musical notes," Violet said. "I thought you said it was a fairy lure."

"It is," Sprite said. "Pixies love music. We just play the notes on a flute. Then the pixie is lured right to us."

Sprite paused. "You have a flute, don't you?"

Violet thought. Then she went to her closet. "I have this," she said. She took out a recorder, a kind of short plastic flute. "We learned how to play it in school."

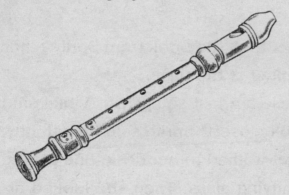

"That'll do!" Sprite said. "Now play! Play!" Excited, he flew in circles.

Violet studied the musical notes. She thought she knew how to play them.

Violet put the recorder to her lips. She put her fingers over the holes. And she blew.

*Squeak!*

Sprite covered his ears with his hands.

"Maybe you should try again," he said.

"I just need practice," Violet said.

Violet played the first note. Then the second. She played the notes one at a time, slowly.

Sprite took his hands from his ears.

"Not bad," he said. "Play it again."

Violet played the tune again, a little faster. This time it sounded kind of pretty.

"Again!" Sprite said. He did a little dance in the air.

Violet played the tune again.

Just as she played the last note, a fairy appeared.

It wasn't Fixit!

Violet stopped playing. She stared at the fairy.

She was twice as tall as Sprite. Her dark hair stuck out wildly from her head. She wore a dress covered with mixed-up letters and numbers.

The fairy folded her arms and stared at Violet.

"So," she said. "What do you want?"

## Chapter Six
# Rusella

Violet didn't know what to say.

She was expecting Fixit! She had no idea who *this* fairy was.

The fairy tapped her foot on the floor. "Can we make this quick?" she asked. "I've got work to do."

Violet found her voice. "Who are you?" she asked.

The fairy rolled her eyes. "You mean you

got me all the way over here and you don't even know who I am?"

Violet nodded.

"My name's Rusella," she said. "And now I've got to get back to the telephone company. I'm busy — "

"Rusella!" Sprite cried. "I know you. You're a message gremlin."

"That's right," Rusella said.

"What's a message gremlin?" Violet asked.

Sprite darted around the room, excited. "Message gremlins like to mix up messages people send to one another," Sprite said. "Like when you think you're supposed to meet your friend in the park, but your friend is waiting for you at the mall."

Violet turned to Rusella. "It's you! You've been causing all the trouble around here. You made me late for Brittany's party. You made the lunch ladies make applesauce stew."

Rusella smiled. "That was a good one, wasn't it? But you haven't seen anything yet."

"What do you mean? What are you up to, Rusella?" Sprite asked worriedly.

Rusella got a dreamy look in her eyes. "When I'm done with this town, it will be a mess! People won't be able to send messages to one another on the phone. Or by e-mail. All the messages will be wrong! Everyone will fight and yell at one another. It's going to be great!"

Rusella looked into Violet's eyes. "And when I'm through with this town, I'm going to mess up the whole human world!"

"Sprite, quick!" Violet yelled. "Look in the *Book of Tricks*! We have to trick her!"

Rusella frowned. "Trick me? Sorry. That's not going to happen."

The gremlin took some pixie dust out of her pocket. She sprinkled it on her head.

Then *poof*! She vanished.

"No!" Violet cried.

Sprite read the *Book of Tricks*. "It's okay, Violet," he said. "We wouldn't have been able to trick her anyway. See — here."

Violet looked in the book. Then she read the rhyme:

*"Rusella's mixed-up messages*
*Are annoying for sure.*
*A bowl of alphabet soup*
*Is the only real cure!"*

"Alphabet soup?" Violet asked. "How are we supposed to do that?"

Just then Leon walked into the room.

"It's time for dinner," he said. He rubbed his stomach. "I'm hungry. I couldn't eat any of that lunch. It was so gross!"

"Lunch!" Sprite cried. "Yes, that's it!"

Sprite quickly took the *Book of Tricks* from Violet. "It's got to be in here somewhere," he said.

"What are you looking for?" Violet asked.

Sprite flipped through the pages. Finally, he smiled.

"It's right here! I knew it!" he said. He looked up from the book. "There are lots of silly rules to follow in the Otherworld. All pixies have to obey them."

"You mean there's a rule that a fairy has to eat alphabet soup?" Violet asked.

"Not exactly," Sprite said. "But a fairy can't turn down an invitation to a meal. We could invite Rusella to lunch. . . ."

"And serve her alphabet soup!" Violet chimed in.

"Who's Rusella?" Leon asked.

Violet and Sprite quickly explained what had happened.

"I get it," Leon said. "But I thought we were trying to trick that angry elf guy."

"We can use this to trick Fixit, too!" Violet said. "Maybe he'll like being invited to lunch. Maybe it will make him smile."

Leon shrugged. "Why not? Lunch makes me smile — if it's pizza."

Violet turned to Sprite. "You're a genius, Sprite. You must have been paying attention in Royal Pixie Tricker class."

Sprite's green cheeks blushed.

"It was nothing," Sprite said. "Now let's get this plan into action!"

# Chapter Seven
## A Tricky Invitation

After dinner, Violet and Leon made the lunch invitations. Violet made the one for Rusella. She drew flowers and butterflies all over the front. Inside, she wrote:

*Dear Rusella,*

*Please come to lunch at my house on Saturday at 12:00. Meet us under the old oak tree.*

*Sincerely,*

*Violet, Sprite, and Leon (my cousin)*

> Dear Rusella,
> Please come to lunch at my house on Saturday at 12:00. Meet us under the old oak tree.
>
> Sincerely,
> Violet, Sprite, and Leon
>
>   (my cousin)

Sprite wanted to know why they couldn't have the lunch right away.

"We have to do it Saturday," Violet explained. "We can't invite two pixies to eat with us in the school lunchroom."

"I guess," Sprite said.

Leon finished up Fixit's invitation. He drew two robots fighting on the front.

"What kind of an invitation is that?" Violet asked.

"Robots are cool," Leon said. "Plus, maybe it will remind Fixit that he needs to fix my robot."

Leon took his toy robot from his pocket. "Hug me, Mommy!" the robot said. Then it sucked its metal thumb.

Violet took the invitation from Leon. "It's fine," she said. "Now we've got to deliver them."

"No problem," Sprite said. He took out some pixie dust from his bag and sprinkled it on Rusella's invitation.

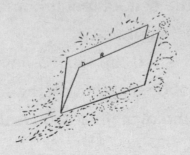

"To Rusella!" Sprite cried. The invitation disappeared.

"Hey, that's cool," Leon said. "I thought that only worked with people."

"It's how pixies send mail," Sprite said. Then he sprinkled pixie dust on the other invitation.

"To Fixit!"

The second invitation vanished.

"Now what do we do?" Leon asked.

"We wait," Violet said. "And hope that those pixies don't cause any more trouble!"

## Chapter Eight
# Bad Manners

But Fixit and Rusella were busy over the next three days.

Fixit ruined more toys with his special magic. All over town, Violet saw teddy bears filled with jelly instead of stuffing. Toy trucks with square wheels. Action figures that couldn't move. It was terrible.

And Rusella spread mixed-up messages all over town.

Violet's mom was late and missed a dentist appointment.

Violet's dad was a musician. He played his guitar in a different place each night. But he showed up at the wrong place three nights in a row!

Each day, Ms. Rose gave them homework. And each day, the kids in the class did the wrong homework.

The whole town was falling apart!

Violet was busy, too.

She asked her mom to go to the store and buy a can of alphabet soup.

She talked to Sprite to find out what other food fairies like.

She found pixie-sized dishes in her toy box.

"Maybe tricking the pixies will be nice

this time," Violet told Sprite. "A fairy lunch could be kind of fun."

"Maybe," Sprite said. But he didn't look so sure.

By Saturday morning, Violet couldn't wait to trick the pixies.

"I hope this works," Violet told Sprite and Leon as they set up the lunch table. "Fixit and Rusella are driving me crazy!"

Violet stepped back from the table, pleased. The table was set with normal cups, plates, and bowls for Violet and Leon. There were tiny cups and plates for Sprite, Fixit, and Rusella.

With Sprite's help, Violet had made a tiny pie out of rose petals and honey.

"Fairies love it!" Sprite said.

There was also a bowl of Beastie Bites

breakfast cereal. It was Sprite's favorite human food.

Then Violet had cut a piece of cheese into two big cubes and three tiny cubes. She put one on each plate.

Sprite licked his lips. "I haven't seen a meal this yummy since I was in the Otherworld!" he said.

Leon didn't look so happy. "Can't we just have pizza?"

Just then, Violet's mom walked out into the yard. She carried a crock of steaming soup.

Sprite quickly hid inside a cup.

"Here's your alphabet soup," Mrs. Briggs said cheerfully.

She put the soup on the table. Then she ruffled Leon's hair. "I think it's so cute that you and Violet are having a little tea party out here."

Leon's freckled cheeks turned red. He looked like he wanted to sink into the ground.

Violet looked at her mom's watch. It was almost twelve o'clock.

"Thanks, Mom," Violet said. "Uh, we need to start now."

"Of course," Mrs. Briggs said. "I'll leave you alone."

Violet and Leon sat down and waited for something to happen.

They didn't have to wait long. There was a *poof*! — and then Rusella appeared.

"Hi," Violet said, trying to act natural. "We're just waiting for Fixit."

"Fairy rules say I have to eat lunch with

you," Rusella said. "They don't say I have to wait. Let's eat!"

Rusella dove right into the food. She picked up a tiny plate and ate the hunk of cheese. Then she picked up the other plates and ate that cheese, too.

"Hey!" Sprite said.

Next Rusella picked up the rose petal pie. She stuffed the whole thing into her mouth.

"Wow! If I ate like that, Mom would ground me for a week," Leon whispered to Violet.

Rusella hopped next to the bowl of Beastie Bites. She popped piece after piece of cereal into her mouth.

Then Rusella burped.

"That was delicious!" she said. "And now I have to be going."

"Don't go yet!" Violet said. "You haven't had your soup."

"Great!" Rusella said. "I'm still hungry!"

Rusella hopped up onto the crock of soup. She leaned over and started scooping the soup into her mouth.

"Mmmm," she said. "This is good."

Then Violet saw Rusella's smile turn to a look of horror.

"What's this?" she asked, looking at her hands. "Noodles shaped like letters? It can't be!"

"It's alphabet soup," Violet said. "We made it just for you!"

"No!" Rusella hopped down. She pushed over the crock of soup. But it was too late.

A tunnel of wind appeared in the air. The swirling wind sucked Rusella into the tunnel.

"Next time I'm having chicken noodle!" Rusella yelled.

And then she disappeared.

"We did it!" Violet cried. "Sprite, look in the book."

Sprite opened up the *Book of Tricks*. A picture of Rusella began to appear on the once-blank page. Violet knew that meant

Rusella's mixed-up messages
Are annoying for sure.
A bowl of alphabet soup
Is the only real cure!

that Rusella was back in the Otherworld. For sure.

Before they could celebrate, there was another *poof*!

Fixit appeared on the tabletop.

"Okay, I'm here," said the elf. "Now where's lunch?"

Violet looked at the table in dismay. Alphabet soup was spilled everywhere. Rusella had eaten all the cheese. And the pie. And the cereal.

"Oh, Fixit, I'm sorry," she said. "You see, Rusella was here, and — "

"That does it!" Fixit said, fuming. "You invite me here and you don't even have any food?"

"Well, you were late," Leon said boldly.

"Impossible," Fixit said. "In fact, I'm early. The invitation said one o'clock."

"One o'clock?" Sprite asked, confused. "But lunch started at twelve."

"It must have been Rusella," Violet said. "She mixed up the message."

Fixit's face was red with rage. "I've had it with you ungrateful children!" he yelled. "I'm going back to Tiny's Toy Store. And when I'm through, I'll make sure no child plays with a toy ever again!"

And then the angry elf vanished in a cloud of pixie dust.

## Chapter Nine
# A Toy for Fixit

Violet thought she might cry. "We were so close!" she said. "I don't know how we're ever going to make Fixit smile. He's the most miserable creature I've ever seen."

"It's okay, Violet," Sprite said, flying in front of her face. "We did get Rusella. That makes six pixies tricked!"

"Actually," Leon said, "I kind of liked Rusella. She was funny."

Violet sighed. "We've got to think of a way to trick Fixit. How can we make him smile?"

"I still think we should tickle him," Sprite suggested. "That always makes *me* smile."

"Something tells me that would only make Fixit angrier," Violet said.

"Yeah," Leon said. "Plus, I wouldn't tickle that guy with a ten-foot pole."

"Maybe the fairy queen can help," Violet suggested.

"It's worth a try," Sprite said. He took a purple jewel from his bag. Queen Mab had talked to them through the jewel before. She had helped them figure out how to trick Aquamarina, Bogey Bill, and Buttercup.

Violet held the jewel in her hand. "Please help us," she whispered.

As if in answer, the jewel began to glow with purple light. Then Queen Mab's face appeared in the jewel.

"Hello, Violet," she said in her musical voice. "I understand you need help tricking Fixit."

Violet nodded. She was usually speechless whenever she saw the beautiful queen.

Queen Mab smiled. "To make Fixit happy,

you must first find out what makes him un-happy."

"How do we do that?" Sprite asked.

But the queen's picture faded. The jewel stopped glowing.

Sprite sighed. "I'm more confused than before," he said. "This is so hard."

"Maybe not," Violet said. "The queen said we have to find out what makes Fixit un-happy. He already told us that."

"Yeah," Leon said. "He's mad at us un-grateful children."

"Right," said Violet. "So what can we do to show that we're grateful?"

"How about sending a thank-you note?" Leon suggested.

"Hmm. Maybe," Violet said.

"How about a present?" asked Sprite. "I love presents!"

"That's a great idea!" Violet said. "We can make him a toy. A toy of his very own."

Violet, Leon, and Sprite got to work. Leon dug up some old wheels and boxes in his room. Violet got some paint and glitter. She found a box of buttons, yarn, and plastic jewels that she had saved. She also got her collection of small plastic toy animals.

They worked all afternoon. They attached the wheels to the boxes. They strung the boxes together with yarn to make a train. Then they decorated the train cars and put the toy animals inside.

"It's a circus train!" Violet said when it was done. "It's beautiful, isn't it?"

"It is pretty nice," Leon said.

Sprite hopped into one of the cars. "Can I go for a ride?" he asked.

"Sorry, Sprite," Violet said. "We'd better get this to Fixit. Fast."

"Right," Sprite said. "How are we going to find him?"

"Fixit said something about Tiny's Toy Store," Violet said. "That's in the mall."

Sprite sprinkled some pixie dust on them.

In a flash, they were in the mall, in front of the toy shop.

"I know Fixit will be happy when he sees this," Violet said, holding up the toy train.

Suddenly, the train flew out of Violet's hands.

"No!" Violet yelled.

She couldn't stop it. The train smashed against the wall. Then it fell to the floor.

Violet ran to the toy train. It was in pieces.

Their present for Fixit was ruined!

## Chapter Ten
# Spoiler Tries to Spoil Things

Violet heard a familiar cackle. She spun around.

A pixie appeared out of nowhere. She had two ponytails and wore a yellow outfit.

"Spoiler!" Violet cried. "Not again!"

Not long ago, Spoiler had tried to stop them from tricking a gremlin named Jolt.

"Finn the Wizard says hello!" Spoiler said. She laughed meanly. Then she vanished.

"Oh, dear," Sprite said. "I didn't know

Spoiler was working for Finn. That's very bad. Very bad indeed."

Violet looked at the broken train. "I give up. What are we going to do now?"

Just then, Fixit popped his head out of the toy-shop door.

"Get in here!" he demanded. "You're causing a commotion."

Violet, Leon, and Sprite followed Fixit to the back of the store.

"You're going to ruin things for me here," the elf scolded. "Can't you just leave me alone?"

"I'm sorry," Violet said. "We were just trying to bring you a present. And then Spoiler came and — "

"A present?" Fixit asked. "For me?"

Violet handed him the toy train. "Sorry. It's broken," she said. "Now you'll be angrier than ever."

But Fixit looked at the train in wonder. His eyes grew wide.

"Did you — did you make this?" he asked.

Violet nodded.

"I helped, too," Leon piped up.

Fixit sat down.

"I can't believe it," he said.

"Don't be angry," Sprite said. "It's not our fault it's broken."

Fixit ignored him.

"I can't believe that children made *me* a present," he said. "A toy just for me. A beautiful, wonderful toy!"

And then Fixit did something amazing.

He smiled.

The wind tunnel appeared. The breeze blew the cap off Fixit's head.

Suddenly, Violet felt sorry for the elf.

"Oh, Fixit!" Violet said. "We would have made you a toy even if we didn't need to trick you. Honest!"

Fixit's smile grew wider. "I believe you!" he said as the tunnel sucked him in. "Thank you! I'll never forget youuuuuuu!"

Fixit and the wind tunnel disappeared.

Sprite opened the *Book of Tricks.*

Violet looked at the brand-new picture of Fixit. She touched the picture.

"Good-bye, Fixit," she said. "I'll never forget you, either!"

## Chapter Eleven
# Halfway There

Later that night, Violet and Sprite went to Leon's room.

"Okay," Violet said. "So far, we've tricked seven pixies."

"Hey, we're halfway there!" Leon said. "We only have seven more to go."

"Right," Violet said. "Sprite, what do we know about them?"

"We've been looking for Hinky Pink since the beginning," Sprite said.

"And there's Spoiler," Leon said. "She really gets on my nerves."

Sprite flew in a circle, like he always did when he was nervous.

"Don't forget Finn the Wizard!" Sprite said. "He worries me most of all."

"He worries me, too," Violet said. "I think we're getting pretty good at tricking pixies. . . ."

"Thanks to me," Leon said.

"Thanks to all of us," Violet said. "But are we good enough to trick Finn?"

Sprite slowly settled onto Violet's shoulder.

"I'm not sure, Violet," he said. "But I'll bet we find out soon!"

# Pixie Tricks Stickers

Place the stickers in the *Book of Tricks*. You can find your very own copy of the *Book of Tricks* in the first two books of the Pixie Tricks series, *Sprite's Secret* and *The Greedy Gremlin*. When Sprite and Violet catch a pixie, stick its sticker in the book. Follow the directions in the *Book of Tricks* to complete each pixie's page. (Pixie Secret: Most of these pixies haven't been caught yet. Save their stickers to use later.)

# ·:ÞIXIE·:ÞRICKS·:·

## Seeing Is Believing!

Available wherever you buy books, or use this order form.

| | | |
|---|---|---|
| ☐ BFB 0-439-17218-7 | **#1: Sprite's Secret** | $3.99 U.S. |
| ☐ BFB 0-439-17219-5 | **#2: The Greedy Gremlin** | $3.99 U.S. |
| ☐ BFB 0-439-17978-5 | **#3: The Pet Store Sprite** | $3.99 U.S. |
| ☐ BFB 0-439-07980-7 | **#4: The Halloween Goblin** | $3.99 U.S. |
| ☐ BFB 0-439-17981-5 | **#5: The Angry Elf** | $3.99 U.S. |

**visit us at www.scholastic.com**